To Yolanda Bunting
—*E.B.*

To Fiore Custode
—*W.M.*

# EVE BUNTING

## PAINTINGS BY WENDELL MINOR

# We Were There

## A NATIVITY STORY

CLARION BOOKS ◆ NEW YORK

*I* am SNAKE.

I sleep when it is cold,

but not tonight.

Tonight I cross the wintry desert.

The curving snake of sand that follows me

shows where I have been.

Soon I will be there.

*I* am TOAD.

Fat, warty,

rough.

My toes have webs between.

But I can leap small leaps

and crawl

and sprawl.

I will be there.

*I* am SCORPION.
I clatter over rocks,
through black ravines,
my curved tail
up and forward on my back.
I will not use my sting tonight.
I will be there.

*I* am COCKROACH.

Shiny, shelled.

I've known the hiding places of the earth

since time began.

I will be there.

I am BAT.
I swoop,
dark-shadowed,
in a loop
of silence.
I do not need the light of that new star
to show me where.
I will be there.

*I* am SPIDER.
I spin my webs
and hang
on shimmering threads
that carry me
from tamarisk to olive tree.
I'm fast,
especially if there is
wind.

$\mathcal{A}$nd if there is no wind
and if there are
no trees
on that bleak hill,
I'll walk.
I'll follow them.
I will be there.

*I* am RAT.

Colorless

as darkening dirt.

I know this inn.

Nightly I scrabble on the floor for scraps.

I squeeze beneath the door tonight.

I slide through stable straw.

And I am there.

*I*n times to come
they'll talk
about this silent night,
the donkey
and the cows,
so generous to share their place.

The little lambs
as soft
as lilies of the field.
The woman,
swollen,
waiting.

$N$o one will look
beyond the light
to darkness
and the corner where we watch,
unwatched.
They will not know
or care.

But we were there.

Clarion Books
a Houghton Mifflin Company imprint
215 Park Avenue South, New York, NY 10003
Text copyright © 2001 by Eve Bunting
Illustrations copyright © 2001 by Wendell Minor

The text was set in 18-point Centaur with Shelly Allegro initial caps.
The illustrations were painted in gouache and watercolors on cold-press watercolor board.

Book design by Wendell Minor.

For information about permission to reproduce selections from this book, write to
Permissions, Houghton Mifflin Company, 215 Park Avenue South, New York, NY 10003.

www.houghtonmifflinbooks.com

Printed in the U.S.A.

*Library of Congress Cataloging-in-Publication Data*

Bunting, Eve, 1928–
We were there / Eve Bunting ; paintings by Wendell Minor.
p.   cm.
Summary: A snake, scorpion, toad, bat, cockroach, spider, and rat tell how they witnessed the birth of the Christ Child.
ISBN 0-395-82265-3
I. Jesus Christ—Nativity—Juvenile fiction. [1. Jesus Christ—Nativity—Fiction. 2. Animals—Fiction.] I. Minor, Wendell, ill. II. Title.

PZ7.B91527 Wg 2001
[E]—dc21     00-065731

BVG 10 9 8 7 6 5 4 3 2 1